Blimey! I'm a Budgie!

A SWOPPERS STORY
by Tony Bradman

BLOOMSBURY
CHILDREN'S
BOOKS

For Hills Trust Primary School . . .
Govan's finest!

First published in Great Britain in 1998
Bloomsbury Publishing Plc, 38 Soho Square, London, WIV 5DF

Copyright © Text Tony Bradman 1998
Copyright © Illustrations Clive Scruton 1998

The moral right of the author has been asserted
A CIP catalogue record of this book is available from the
British Library

ISBN 0 7475 3572 8

10 9 8 7 6 5 4 3 2 1

Text Design by Dorchester Typesetting Group Ltd
Cover Design by Michelle Radford
Printed in Great Britain by Clays Ltd, St Ives plc

Contents

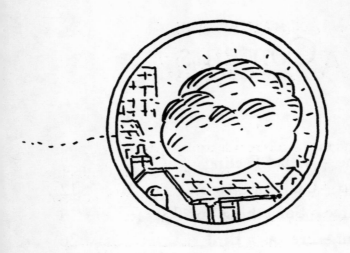

A small cloud of gas drifts towards an average town . . .
It shimmers, and gives off an eerie glow.
Where it came from is a mystery. Perhaps it has
travelled across the unimaginable chasms of space.
Perhaps it is the product of a secret laboratory . . .
Whatever the truth, one thing is certain. Any
child who meets it is in for an amazing experience,
as a particular boy is about to discover.
Follow him as he tumbles into the weird, wild
and wonderful world of ... **Swoppers!**

CHAPTER ONE
A Bad Feeling

'What do you mean you're not walking home with me?' said Adam, whirling angrily to face Craig, his best friend. Adam's stomach had tightened into a knot of worry. 'But we *always* walk home together!'

The two boys were surrounded by the familiar end-of-the-day junior cloakroom chaos. Noisy children were grabbing coats and schoolbags and lunchboxes, glad it was Friday and the long week finally over.

'I told you this morning, remember?' said Craig, looking at Adam with a puzzled expression. 'My dad's bringing the car, and he's taking me into town to get some new shoes. I don't see what the problem is.'

'It doesn't matter,' Adam muttered, his cheeks suddenly feeling very warm. He pushed past his friend, went out of the door, and stomped off into the playground. Craig soon appeared at his elbow, though.

'Listen, Adam,' Craig said. 'Are you OK?'

'I'm fine,' snapped Adam, speeding up. 'Why wouldn't I be?'

'I don't know, do I?' Craig replied, breaking into a trot. 'But you have to admit you've been acting pretty strangely recently. To say the least.'

'Isn't that your dad?' said Adam. His friend turned towards the dense crowd of adults and children beyond the fence. While Craig was distracted, Adam slipped through the gate and into the press of bodies.

'Adam, wait!' he heard Craig yelling. But Adam ignored him.

Adam walked on, dodging pushchairs and whiny little brothers and sisters and yapping dogs straining at leads and dawdling, gossiping grown-ups. Eventually the crowd thinned, and he reached the corner.

As a rule, Adam and Craig would cross there with the lollipop lady. Then they'd go the long way home so they could visit their favourite sweet-shop. But tonight Adam decided to take the shortest route possible.

He glanced nervously over his shoulder, and hurried down the road.

There was no sign of Kenny yet, thank goodness. Kenny's teacher Miss Wilson was a bit daffy, and quite often the last to let her class out. But Adam couldn't rely on that, and definitely didn't plan on hanging around.

The sooner he was safely at home, the better.

As he walked quickly along the street, Adam thought about Kenny. The word in the playground was that Kenny had trouble at home. But Adam was in a different class, and had never had much to do with him, anyway.

Until recently, that is. One playtime a few weeks

ago, Adam had noticed Kenny staring at him. From that moment on, wherever Adam went in the playground, Kenny was there, too. You couldn't miss him, either.

Kenny seemed very big to Adam, who was small for his age.

This week, Kenny had made a point of sitting next to Adam at lunch every day. Then yesterday, Kenny had bumped into Adam in the corridor, almost knocking him down. It was obvious he'd done it deliberately.

And today Kenny had cornered him in the toilets. Alone.

'I, er . . . I want a word with you after school,' Kenny had said. That was all. But it had given Adam a bad feeling. A very bad feeling indeed.

Adam started to run. He ran faster, and faster, and faster, his eyes fixed on the huge oak tree that stood near his house, his heavy schoolbag banging rhythmically on his back as his feet slapped the hard pavement.

Eventually, a painful stitch in his side forced him to slow to a walk. He came to the low wall of his own front garden, and sat there. He was totally puffed out – but he'd made it, he thought. He'd actually made it.

Suddenly he heard footsteps. Adam raised his head – and saw Kenny looming above him! It must have been one of Miss Wilson's good days, Adam thought, bitterly. Kenny had probably hidden behind the oak tree.

'I've been waiting for you,' said Kenny. For a brief instant, Adam thought Kenny seemed rather nervous himself. 'We, er . . . need to talk.'

'W-what about?' said Adam. He stood up, hesitantly.

'The money you owe me,' said Kenny, growing more confident.

'But I don't owe you any money,' said Adam.

'You do *now*,' said Kenny, putting on a scowl, and moving closer . . .

CHAPTER TWO
Under a Shadow

'Well, I don't know,' said Adam's Mum, scraping his half-eaten breakfast into the bin. 'It's not like you to leave any food on your plate. I hope you're not sickening for something. There's a nasty bug doing the rounds.'

'I'm just not hungry, Mum,' Adam mumbled, keeping his eyes down.

'Umm . . . I'll let you off – *this* time,' said Mum, putting his plate in the dishwasher. 'But you're not yourself, are you? Maybe I'll take you to the doctor on Monday. Anyway, come on. Your gran's expecting us.'

It was Saturday, the day Mum and Adam usually went to see his gran. A few minutes later they were walking to her house. Mum chattered away, casually slipping in the occasional probing question, hoping to find out what was wrong.

But Adam wouldn't say much. He didn't want to be drawn out, and he didn't want to tell any more lies, either. The truth was that he *did* feel sick, although it certainly wasn't the kind of sickness you got from a bug.

It had more to do with that knot of worry in his stomach. Since his conversation with Kenny, the knot had been getting tighter, and tighter . . .

Adam already had an appointment set for Monday morning. He was supposed to meet Kenny before school started – and give him some money. Kenny hadn't said what would happen if Adam didn't show up.

Kenny didn't need to go into detail. Adam knew the score.

He had a very strong imagination, too, so he hadn't slept well last night, what with Kenny chasing him through every dream. Adam had woken up

sweating . . . twice. Suddenly he realised they had
arrived at Gran's.

Mum rang the bell, and a smiling gran opened the
door.

'Hello!' she said, her smile turning into a look of
concern. 'Oh dear, who's this with a face like a wet
weekend? Not my Sunny Jim, surely?'

'Hi, Gran,' he said, and kissed her. 'Is it OK if I
watch TV?'

'Of course it is, sweetheart,' said Gran, glancing at
Mum with raised eyebrows. Mum replied with an I-
Haven't-Got-A-Clue shrug. 'Your Mum and I can
have a nice cup of tea – and a talk. I'll put the
kettle on.'

Gran and Mum went into the kitchen, while Adam trudged into the front room. He found the remote, and huddled in the corner of the sofa.

Adam zapped from channel to channel until he found an old *Road Runner* cartoon. But he couldn't concentrate on Wile E. Coyote's endless, futile attempts to catch his prey. Adam had far too much on his mind.

What should he *do*? If he gave in to Kenny on Monday, Adam knew it would only be the beginning. His life would be a misery from then on. But if he didn't . . . Kenny was bound to make his life a misery in any case.

Whichever way he looked at it, Adam felt utterly doomed. Gran said she called him her Sunny Jim because he was always such a happy boy. But Sunny Jim was definitely under a shadow now, he thought.

Just then, Gran's pet budgie Sparky chirped at Adam from the table behind the sofa. Adam turned to look at the little bird in his cage. Sparky tipped his head to one side, chirped cheerily at Adam again, and spoke.

'Keep your pecker *up!*' he squawked.

'Huh!' grunted Adam. Sparky peered intently at him. 'That's all right for *you* to say,' Adam

murmured. 'You don't have any problems.'

Adam sighed, deeply. He'd thought of something else, too. At that moment, Mum was probably asking Gran if she'd help find out what was wrong – and Mum and Gran together made a tough team of interrogators.

But Adam knew he didn't want to talk about Kenny to *anybody*.

Adam hit the standby button on the remote and

went to the kitchen. As he pushed open the door, Mum and Gran paused in their conversation.

'All right, love?' said Gran. 'Would you like a drink?'

'No thanks, Gran,' Adam replied. 'Mum, can I go round to Craig's for a while? He's, er . . . got this new computer game he wants to show me.'

Craig only lived in the next street, so Adam knew Mum wouldn't mind. He promised to be home for tea, and left. But once he was outside, Adam strode off in the *opposite* direction from his friend's house . . .

And straight towards the biggest adventure of his life.

CHAPTER THREE
Something Spooky

Adam brooded as he walked, his thoughts circling round and round an image of Kenny. He barely noticed where his feet were taking him, until at last he realised he was approaching the huge oak tree near his house.

The street was deserted, and strangely quiet, almost as if it were waiting for something spooky to happen. Adam found himself thinking. He stopped, and stood moodily near the tree. He had never, ever felt so low.

How he wished he wasn't weighed down by his problem! If only he could have a simple life like Sparky's, with absolutely nothing to worry him. A vision of Gran's cheery, chirpy pet filled Adam's mind . . .

And at precisely that instant, a certain small cloud of gas wafted up, swiftly enfolding Adam in its shifting, wispy coils. He watched in wonder as the eerily shimmering mist twisted and curled before his eyes.

But Adam's wonder quickly changed to anxiety. It occurred to him the cloud might be some kind of potentially poisonous pollution, an idea which made him rather nervous. He decided to walk on a little further . . .

And that's when things got *seriously* bizarre.

To his horror, Adam discovered he was unable to move a single muscle. He couldn't use his legs or his arms, and he couldn't turn his head or close his eyes. He couldn't even open his mouth to scream for help.

Although he was certainly doing plenty of screaming inside.

Then the strangest *sucking* sensation started in his stomach. Soon it seemed to be powerfully pulling every part of him inwards. It grew stronger, and

stronger, until Adam's body was quivering uncontrollably.

At the same time there was the weirdest *emptying* sensation, too. He couldn't describe it any other way. It began in his fingers and toes and seemed to spread through his bones, hollowing them out from the inside.

Adam suddenly felt as if he were incredibly *light*.

As the sucking reached unbearable intensity, the quivering suddenly ceased. Then something seemed to *SNAP!* in his stomach, releasing the tension and catapulting him into the air with a *TWANNING!*

Adam *WHOOSHED!* skywards like a rocket, narrowly missing a branch of the oak tree, and hurtled up into the wild blue yonder. But he soon slowed

down, until at least he hung ominously motionless
for an instant . . .

Then started to fall, gathering momentum until
he was plunging towards the distant Earth below at
incredible speed, accompanied by a whistling sound

– *WHEEEEEE!* – that made him think of a bomb dropping.

And Adam knew what happened when bombs landed.

He braced himself for the agonising, explosive *SPLAT!* that would mean his end . . . but it didn't come. Whatever he finally hit was quite soft, although his landing did knock the breath out of him. *OOOOOF!*

But there was more in store. Amazingly, Adam's head seemed to be changing shape. His eyes were forced further and further apart, while his nose and mouth scrunched themselves into the very centre of his face.

His ears simply vanished, and his chest puffed out with a *POP!*

His skin started to tingle terribly, and he began to hear creepy *RUSTLING* and *CREAKING* sounds which grew louder, and louder and turned into a *SWISH!* that set him on his feet and sent him spinning . . .

He came to a halt at last, but then he began swaying and staggering, like a boxer who's almost been knocked out. He was very dizzy, and he felt pretty sick, and he didn't even seem able to *see* properly any more.

Vast areas of brown and green and blue swung round him in two great, overlapping arcs. Adam tried to concentrate, and an area of crumbly, black blobs swam into focus. A pair of pink prongy things appeared, too.

Adam stared at them, then at the spindly legs they were attached to. The legs merged into a plump-looking body covered in fine blue feathers. And somehow he seemed able to see a tail of long feathers behind him . . .

Adam paused for a second. He raised an arm and glanced along it. He did the same with the other . . . and realised that now they were – *WINGS!*

'Blimey! I'm a budgie!' he thought – and keeled over backwards.

CHAPTER FOUR

Free as a Bird

Adam lay there without moving for a few seconds, desperately trying to get his emotions under control. He closed his eyes and told himself that none of what he'd just experienced could actually have happened.

People don't turn into budgies, he thought. Maybe he was having a nightmare brought on by worrying about Kenny. Yes, that was it. He was dreaming, and hadn't even got up yet, or gone to Gran's with Mum . . .

But then he realised there was one major problem with that theory – he didn't *feel* as if he were dreaming. The ground was soft and damp beneath him, and he could hear leaves rustling in the breeze somewhere nearby.

No, Adam decided, he was definitely wide awake. He was pretty sure he hadn't suddenly gone barmy, either. He knew who he was – he could remember his address and phone number – so what had been going on?

Adam ran the memory of the last few minutes through his mind like a videotape on fast forward. The weird stuff had started when that eerie, shimmering cloud had appeared out of nowhere and swallowed him.

And he *had* been thinking about Sparky at that exact moment, hadn't he? So perhaps the cloud *was* some kind of toxic, polluted fog which turned you into whatever was in your mind when you encountered it.

It was crazy, it was impossible – but it was the only logical explanation!

Adam rolled over, awkwardly spread his wings, and clumsily hopped on to his prongy feet in a flurry of feathers. The more he thought about it, the more

he realised that he really did feel small, and well . . .
budgie-like.

He opened his eyes – and nearly fell over again. Those
vast overlapping arcs of brown and green and blue
instantly started swinging round his head, and he felt
even more sick than before. Then it dawned on him.

This was how budgies saw the world.

He stood very still, and concentrated even harder,
and soon he began to make a little more sense of

what he was seeing. Each of his eyes took in a huge area, and together they gave him an almost circular field of vision.

It would have been overwhelming if he hadn't soon realised he could sort of *zoom* in on smaller areas, or details. He must have done that instinctively when he'd looked at his feet and legs, and his . . . er, wings.

Gradually, the brown and the green and the blue resolved themselves into a *colossal* oak tree, its giant leaves, and immense patches of sky. The crumbly black blobs turned out to be the soil round the base of the tree.

That was obviously what had given him his soft landing, thought Adam, understanding how incredibly lucky he's been. If he'd crashed on to the pavement, he wouldn't simply be a budgie now – he'd be a *dead* budgie.

But he wasn't dead. He was alive, and the panicky part of his mind said he should get to Mum double-quick and communicate with her somehow. She could take him to doctors or scientists who would know what to do.

They might be able to change him back into a human being. He might even manage it himself, he thought, realising with a shock that the strange shimmering in the distance was the cloud slowly wafting away . . .

What if a second close encounter with the gas reversed the process? Maybe he should simply walk into it with an image in his mind of how he looked normally. Adam set off after the cloud – but stopped, immediately.

Another part of his mind had just said something startling. If he didn't get changed back, *he wouldn't have to face Kenny on Monday.*

In fact, he wouldn't have to face Kenny ever again. No more fear in the playground, no more agonising about what to do. A wonderful vision of a happy future rose in Adam's mind, and his spirit soared.

He would be as free as a bird, he realised, and laughed inwardly. He had a brief twinge of conscience when he remembered Mum and Gran, but he quickly smothered it. All that mattered was escaping from Kenny.

Besides, being a budgie might turn out to be a fantastic adventure, he told himself brightly. It wasn't every day you were given this kind of opportunity. Then suddenly, Adam heard a noise, and felt rather uneasy.

Something large was heading in his direction.

CHAPTER FIVE
Running and Flapping

The noise Adam could hear was a kind of *WHIN-ING* that changed to a *HUMMING* as whatever was making it got closer, and closer, and closer. Finally it became a dreadful *ROARING*, and Adam dived behind a thick tree root.

He peeped above it in the direction of the noise, and his beak fell open with amazement. A car as big as an ocean liner was rushing down the road – seemingly straight towards him! Adam ducked, panic-stricken.

But the car flashed past and left a trail of evil-smelling exhaust smoke. Its roar faded to a hum, then a whine, then vanished. Adam coughed and coughed, and for a moment he thought he was going to choke to death.

He did realise the car hadn't been the size of an ocean liner, though. It was a normal car, of course — and had only *seemed* gigantic because he was so small. And he'd probably been reasonably safe beside the tree.

But he didn't feel safe. He felt vulnerable and exposed, especially as the sudden appearance of the car seemed to have broken the spell that had kept the street empty and quiet. Adam could hear a lot more noise.

There was a very loud *BANG!* like a door being slammed, and a *THUMP-THUMP-THUMP* which he felt in his hollow bones as much as heard. It could be somebody walking down a garden path, he thought.

Adam had a sudden vision of being squashed by a giant shoe.

Then that was replaced by another, much nastier image — Adam remembered seeing what a neighbour's cat had done to a bird. She'd only left a few blood-soaked feathers. And that killer cat might still be around . . .

It was time he moved on, Adam decided. He had to find a place to hide until he'd made some plans for his new life as a budgie. He peeked nervously over the root again, and was relieved to see the coast was clear.

He stumbled across the black, crumbly blobs of soil and reached the pavement. It stretched endlessly ahead of him like an airport runway, although he could make out his own huge front gate distantly to one side.

Maybe he could sneak into the back garden and hide in a shed for a while, he thought. He set off, waddling uncertainly along the pavement on his thin, spindly legs – and within seconds he was out of breath.

He wasn't making a great deal of progress, either. The gate seemed as distant as ever. Then he stopped in his tracks, and realised he might be capable of moving more speedily. After all, he was a *bird*, wasn't he?

And birds could fly, he thought. Even budgies.

He lifted both wings and examined them. They seemed to be in working order. But the question was – how did he use them? It seemed the simplest thing would be to do some flapping. It was worth a try, in any case.

Adam flapped cautiously at first, then more strongly, and felt for a second that it might be working. He flapped harder, and harder – but got nowhere. Blast, he thought. There was obviously a lot more to this.

Then he remembered that a moment ago the pavement had reminded him of an airport runway, and he thought about planes. They needed to be moving at quite some speed before they could take off, he realised.

It occurred to him that maybe budgies did too.

Adam started walking again, and flapped at the same time, and soon he was running and flapping,

PUFF! PUFF! PUFF!

and then he began to feel his wings pulling him upwards, and he ran and flapped more and more furiously, until finally . . .

He felt his feet leave the ground, and he knew he was flying.

Adam skimmed above the pavement, and noticed he didn't have to flap quite so hard to keep going. He wondered how he could gain some height, and realised that's what those long feathers on his rear end must be for.

He raised his tail slightly – and suddenly he wasn't just flying. His spirit had soared when he'd contemplated being free of Kenny, and now his

body was soaring as well. Every beat of his wings lifted him higher.

He measured his skyward progress against the oak tree. He was a quarter of the way up, then half-way, then three-quarters, and a few short wing beats later he landed on the topmost branch and gripped it tight.

Then he made the mistake of looking down . . .

CHAPTER SIX

Into Thin Air

Adam's neighbourhood was spread below him like a gigantic satellite picture, and the sight made him sick again. He'd never been afraid of heights before – although he'd never been this small, or this high, either.

Then he realised he was being stupid. After all, he *had* flown up there himself, hadn't he? So he had no reason to think he couldn't just fly back down. And he certainly couldn't stay at the top of an oak tree for ever.

Even if the prospect of jumping into thin air *was* scary.

Oh well, here goes nothing, Adam thought, nervously. He took a deep breath, raised his wings, closed his eyes, and *LEAPT!* from the branch. For a terrifying second he fell . . . and then suddenly, he started to glide.

Adam couldn't believe how wonderful it felt. He opened his eyes and saw that he was descending in a graceful arc. He thought of a hang-glider he'd seen on holiday last year, and tilted a little to correct his course.

He began beating his wings once more, and soon the houses and gardens in his street were racing past beneath him. He tried to pick out his own, but couldn't recognise it from this unfamiliar angle.

Adam dipped down for a better look. He swept over a fence, then realised he was moving very fast – and that he didn't have enough control for this kind of low-level flying. There were too many things to avoid.

He just managed to dodge past a toddler's slide, then a greenhouse loomed at him from behind a large bush. He desperately banked the other way, but still clipped the edge with his left wing tip, spun off course . . .

And found himself hurtling towards a crowded washing line, one of the circular kind that looks like a giant spider's web on a stick. There would be no missing it, either. Adam knew he was on a collision course.

He also had a nasty feeling that getting tangled in the sleeves and straps and folds of the wet clothes might be pretty dangerous for a bird.

So he quickly folded his wings, pressed them close

to his sides, and tucked his beak deep into his chest feathers. Incredibly, he WHIZZED through a series of tiny gaps between the clothes, and shot out unharmed.

But his streamlined shape also increased his speed, and Adam suddenly realised some kind of square, flat surface was dead ahead. Three small, dark figures with their backs to him were perched on the near side.

He *WHOOSHED!* in just over them and *CRASHED!* heavily onto a hard, rough, surface. He slid painfully across it on his front, vaguely aware of loud, panicky squawking and a frantic fluttering of wings behind him.

He finally scraped to a halt, his head poking out

over an edge. Adam giddily sensed an immense emptiness beyond, and glanced downwards. There seemed to be an awful lot of grass rather a long way below.

The square, flat surface was supported by a huge, thick, knobbly pole which rose straight out of a giant X-shaped base. Suddenly Adam knew where he was. He had landed on a bird-table in somebody's garden!

'Well, really!' said a cross voice as Adam carefully got to his feet. Adam, chest feathers were now all ruffled and dirty. 'I suppose you think that was funny.'

Adam turned round and saw three birds flying towards him. They landed together and stood at a distance. One of them was slightly bigger than Adam, one was about his size, and one was slightly smaller.

'I beg your pardon?' said Adam, amazed at what he'd heard.

Adam knew Sparky could speak, and that many parrots and minas could as well. But that was pure imitation. It hadn't occurred to him birds might be able to communicate with each other in their own language.

Or that he would be able to understand him.

'Why, you could give someone a heart attack playing a silly trick like that,' spluttered the biggest bird

in the same voice he had just heard.

'Keep your feathers on, Dottie,' said the middle-sized bird. 'That was no trick, that was an emergency landing. He looks shook up to me, too.'

'Yes, are you all right?' the smallest bird said gently. The three of them hopped a little closer, and peered at Adam with obvious concern.

Luckily, Adam seemed to have fallen amongst friends . . .

CHAPTER SEVEN

Wild Creatures

'I'm fine, thanks,' said Adam at last. The three birds tipped their heads to one side in unison, and waited politely for him to continue. 'And I'm very sorry if I startled you. I, er . . . sort of lost my way there for a second.'

'No problem, mate!' replied the middle-sized bird cheerfully. 'It can happen to the best of us sometimes.' His two companions nodded in agreement. 'Besides, you're not from around here, are you?'

'Er . . . no, I'm not,' Adam replied.

It was a fib, technically speaking. But Adam realised they would find the truth difficult to understand, and decided he wouldn't even try to explain it to them. In any case, his old life was behind him now.

'So nothing . . . *forced* you to make an emergency landing?' said the smallest bird, glancing at the others, who returned her look meaningfully.

'No,' said Adam. Now it was his turn to be confused. 'Why?'

'Oh, no reason,' the smallest bird answered lightly. The three of them seemed rather relieved, Adam thought. 'Well then, we should introduce ourselves,' the smallest bird continued. 'I'm Jen. Pleased to meet you.'

'I'm Buster,' said the middle-sized bird. 'Likewise, I'm sure.'

'And *I* am Dottie,' said the biggest bird, grandly. 'Delighted to make your acquaintance. But tell me . . . what kind of bird *are* you, exactly?'

'I was wondering that too,' added Buster. 'I'm a sparrow, Dottie's a chaffinch, and Jen's a wren. But I've never seen a bird like you before.'

'Oh, Buster!' said Jen, embarrassed. 'You can be so *rude* . . . '

'It's OK,' said Adam. Of course, these were wild creatures, he thought, so they wouldn't get much chance to see birds who were kept indoors as pets. 'I'm a budgie! 'We're a very rare species,' he said, thinking fast.

'Ah, mystery explained,' said Buster. 'Er . . . sorry for being beaky.'

'And I'm sorry for snapping at you,' said Dottie. Adam didn't respond. He was grappling with the idea that 'beaky' in bird language must mean 'nosy'.

'I'm not usually so jumpy, by the way,' Dottie went on. 'It's just . . .'

'Leave it *out*, Dottie,' hissed Buster. 'We said we were going to forget all that and have *fun*, remember? Maybe our new friend would like to play with us.' He turned to Adam. 'What did you say your name was?'

'I didn't, said Adam, suddenly feeling slightly uneasy at this second hint of something troubling them. Then he made himself stop worrying. Their problems were none of his business. 'It's Adam. And you can count me in.'

'That's great, Adam,' said Buster, eagerly hopping forward. 'I'm sure the four of us are going to be *fantastic* together. Now, bags I start. You three can work out between you who takes the lead next, OK? Ready, steady . . .'

'Not so fast, Buster,' said Dottie. Buster paused in mid-flap. 'I'm not going *anywhere* until I've done some preening. And *do* forgive me for mentioning this, but I'm not the only one who needs a bit of tidying up.'

Dottie stared pointedly at Adam's ruffled, dirty front, then dipped her beak into her chest feathers. Buster sighed and rolled his eyes, but did the same to his own. And Jen did the same to hers, rather more delicately.

Adam watched carefully. He realised they were picking out dirt with their beaks and combing their feathers back into place. He copied them, and to his delight, he discovered the whole process was very soothing.

Soon his chest was completely clean, and his feathers were nice and neat and smooth again. He looked round, and saw that Dottie, Buster and Jen had finished their preening, and were patiently waiting for him.

'Listen, I've been thinking,' he said, hesitantly. 'We play lots of games where I come from, but they,

er . . . might not be the same as yours. You don't suppose you could give me a quick run-down, could you?'

'I'd be glad to, mate!' said Buster. 'We usually do Ins-And-Outies first, of course, then Ups-And-Downies, then Tag-My-Tail, then Sneaky-Beak, and then we finish off with Good-Feather-Bad-Feather. Does that help?'

'Er . . . absolutely,' said Adam, who hadn't understood any of it. Buster, Dottie and Jen nodded, raised their wings and dived off the bird-table.

Adam took a deep breath, and followed.

CHAPTER EIGHT
Aerial Acrobatics

Adam had decided he wasn't going to let his new friends think he was stupid. It was bound to be the same here as in the playground, he thought. If you didn't catch on to a game quickly, you weren't asked to play again. And that was the last thing he wanted. So he would simply have to do what he'd done with the preening – observe the others, then copy them. Adam felt reasonably confident, though. He'd always been good at games.

Buster, Dottie and Jen flew swiftly across several gardens, just above hedge height. Adam found it hard to keep up, and was relieved when they slowed down. He realised they were approaching an old wooden fence.

Adam noticed it had holes in it of varying sizes. Some were big enough for a bird to pass through easily, and some would be a tight squeeze. And suddenly Adam had a inkling of what Ins-And-Outies might involve . . .

'Five-Hole-Gap and Ten-Pattern-Tops?' asked

Buster, hovering for a moment. Dottie and Jen shrugged, then nodded. Buster didn't say another word, but whipped round, and dived for the nearest hole in the fence.

He shot through it, then came back through another, and flew in and out of several more. Dottie started her turn when Buster emerged from his fifth hole. So that was what Five-Hole-Gap meant, thought Adam . . .

'Here goes, Adam!' Jen said, happily. 'Best of luck!'

And with a quick flick of her wings, she was gone. Adam counted her through five holes as the rules obviously demanded, then set off towards the fence himself. He was quite nervous, but rather excited, too.

It was as he'd thought. Ins-And-Outies was a kind of aerial acrobatics, and the idea was to try and make the most intricate pattern through the smallest holes.

Ten-Pattern-Tops just meant you only had ten goes.

They went on to Ups-And-Downies next, which was the same as Ins-And-Outies, only through the

holes in the roof of an old shed. Then they moved on to Tag-My-Tail, which was like ordinary tag, but more exciting.

After that they flew back to the fence where they'd started, for Sneaky-Beak. In this, one player stayed out of sight on the far side of the fence, while the others had a sneak through the holes without getting caught.

It was all very enjoyable, thought Adam – but it

was also a great way of learning how to fly properly. In fact, he did so much flying that he really began to feel comfortable with almost every aspect of his budgie body.

He was even getting used to the wide circle of vision, and realised life as a bird would be impossible without it. It had certainly helped him work out the geography of the area. His house was only a few gardens away . . .

He didn't want to think about that, though, just as he didn't want to look closely at the huge, slow-moving figures he glimpsed once or twice in the gardens. His new friends steered well clear of them, and he did too.

He didn't know how he'd feel if one of them turned out to be his mum . . .

'Cheer up, Adam!' said Dottie suddenly, interrupting his thoughts. 'Now for my favourite game. Don't you just love Good-Feather-Bad-Feather?'

'Er . . . of course,' said Adam uncertainly. 'Doesn't everybody?'

He needn't have worried, though. Good-Feather-Bad-Feather was a sort of mad aerial version of Pass-The-Parcel. You had to pass a feather from beak to beak more and more quickly, and it was an

absolute hoot.

'OK, I think I've had enough,' said Adam eventually. He was totally puffed, and weak from laughing so much. 'I have to rest for a while.'

They went back to the garden with the circular washing line and the bird-table where Adam had met his new friends. He landed on it once more, amazed at how much he had developed since their first encounter.

'That was truly *marvellous*,' said Dottie as she landed.

'I couldn't agree more!' said Buster, landing just behind her.

'We haven't had so much fun in *ages*,' said Jen, landing last of all.

'Neither have I,' said Adam happily. He had definitely made the right decision, he thought. His new life as a budgie was *brilliant*. Great friends, loads of fun, but most important – nothing whatsoever to worry about.

Suddenly a shadow fell over him, and the world went dark.

CHAPTER NINE
Razor-like Talons

Adam nervously raised his head – and saw a creature more than twice his size descending from the sky directly above him. Its huge wings were outstretched, and its bright yellow legs fully extended for landing.

The creature THUMPED! on to the bird-table, making it shake. It folded its wings with a great

RUSTLING! of feathers. It let out a breath with a sudden *HISSSSSSSS!* And it slowly lowered its gaze to stare at . . . *Adam!*

Adam gulped. The creature's eyes were far more scary then those of the T-Rex in *Jurassic Park*, he thought. They were black pools the size of car steering-wheels, without pupils or irises, and they were utterly pitiless.

Between them was a big beak that looked viciously sharp and cruel. The creature's powerful body was covered in reddish-brown plumage, and its six toes were tipped with long, wickedly curved, razor-like talons.

Somehow Adam didn't think the creature had come to play.

'Well, well,' the creature said in a deep, gravelly voice that Adam could feel in his bones. He suddenly realised the feathers on the back of his neck were standing up, and his legs were trembling. 'What *do* we have here?'

Adam heard a panic-stricken cheeping behind him, and turned round. Dottie, Buster and Jen were in a tight, quivering huddle, their heads tucked under each other's wings, too scared even to glance at the creature.

'Pssst!' Adam whispered at them, uncomfortably aware that the creature's stare was still boring into his back. 'Who the heck *is* this?'

'It's . . . it's . . . *KONAN THE KESTREL!*' his three friends wailed desperately. 'We're doomed, we're doomed!' We're all going to die!'

'Or course you are, my sweeties . . . eventually,' rumbled Konan. Adam turned to face him again. 'But it's your little blue chum I'm interested in most. If I'm not mistaken, he's a new item on the local menu.'

Adam suddenly went cold from head to tail, and that old, familiar knot of anxiety twisted in his stomach. Konan's meaning was unmistakable. It seemed Adam's new life as a budgie might turn out to be rather short . . .

'Leave him alone, you big bully!' Jen shouted. Adam looked, and saw her bravely peeking out of the huddle. The other two shushed at her, but she wouldn't be silenced. 'He doesn't deserve to be eaten. None of us do!'

'Is that so?' Konan replied – and moved. Adam stiffened as he felt the razor-sharp talons of one large foot sweep past him, very close. Konan stood over the huddle and bent down, his beak almost touching them.

'*AAAAAAAAAAGH!*' they wailed. Jen frantically pulled her head back under a wing, and the three
friends squashed together more tightly.

'I'll be the judge of that, my darlings,' said Konan
softly, then turned to Adam again. 'Now, I've eaten
today, but the question is, am I still hungry? What
do *you* think, you adorable little snack? Do you feel
. . . *lucky?*'

'I d-d-don't know,' said Adam, his heart hammer-
ing in his chest.

'Umm, let me see,' said Konan, suddenly moving
back to his original position. Adam held his breath
as the talons on Konan's other foot swept past him.
'I've had a caterpillar, a mouse, a vole, a juicy
sparrow . . .'

'*EEEEEEK!*' squeaked Buster from the huddle.

'. . . two plump chaffinches, three rather tasty
wrens . . .' now Dottie and Jen added their squeaks
to Buster's. 'So to be honest, I *am* rather full . . .'

'Phew!' sighed Adam quietly to himself.

'. . . at the moment, that is,' Konan said fiercely,
suddenly swivelling with incredible speed until his
beak was a mere feather's thickness from Adam's.
'But you won't be surprised if I'm a bit . . . *peckish*

later, will you?'

Adam stood motionless, transfixed by his reflection in Konan's eyes. He listened to Konan's breathing, and felt the hot gusts gently ruffling the feathers on his head and chest. Time seemed to have stopped . . . *dead.*

'No, I w-w-won't,' Adam said at last.

'Jolly good,' said Konan, straightening up and towering over him. 'I'm glad we understand each other. Anyway, much as I'd like to, I can't stand here chatting all day, so I'll say goodbye. But don't worry – I'll be back.'

With that, Konan spread his vast, dark wings again, and took off.

CHAPTER TEN
Twisted with Fear

Adam stood rooted to the spot, watching Konan climb effortlessly into the sky. The predator gradually grew smaller, and soon became a distant black dot. But Adam didn't relax until the dot had completely disappeared.

Even then, the knot in his stomach stayed twisted with fear.

'Hey, Adam!' Buster whispered, frantically. 'What's *happening*?'

Adam remembered his friends, and slowly turned round. Dottie, Buster and Jen were still huddled tightly together in the same place, and still quivering. They peered at him wide-eyed from beneath their wings.

'It's OK,' said Adam. 'He's gone.'

The huddle broke up, although the three birds stuck very close to each other, anxiously examining the surrounding airspace. At last, with a twittering of relief, they seemed to accept that they were safe – for now.

'I simply cannot believe I survived an encounter with . . . Konan,' said Dottie, twitching as she spoke his name. She closed her eyes, and dramatically held a wing across her brow. 'It was . . . *unspeakable*.'

'Did you hear what he said?' Buster spluttered, utterly outraged. 'He's eaten a-a *sparrow*! I only hope it wasn't anybody I'm related to.'

'All that talk is *typical* of him, too,' said Dottie. 'Devouring small, defenceless creatures isn't enough, oh no. He has to *torment* us as well.'

'I wish the pair of you would be quiet for a second,' Jen snapped. 'Can't you see it was Adam who got the worst of it?' Dottie and Buster fell silent, and the three birds hopped over. 'Did he . . . hurt you?' Jen asked, softly.

'No, he didn't,' Adam replied, his mind filling with images of what those razor-sharp talons and that terrible beak might easily have done to him. Suddenly he felt angry with his friends. 'But why didn't you *tell* me?'

'Er . . . tell you what?' said Buster, trying to sound innocent.

'Oh, nothing much,' said Adam. 'Just that there was a killer kestrel in the area who might drop in unexpectedly – and threaten to *eat* me.'

'Well, we, er . . .' Dottie mumbled, glancing uneasily at the other two.

'I should have guessed something was wrong when you asked me whether I'd been forced to land,' said Adam, 'and when Dottie started talking about being jumpy. Konan's been a problem for a while, hasn't he?'

If it were possible for three small birds to look sheepish, Adam thought, then that's exactly how Dottie, Buster and Jen seemed at that moment. They lowered their heads in embarrassment, and shifted from foot to foot.

'He arrived a couple of months ago,' said Jen eventually and he's terrorised the neighbourhood ever since. But we hadn't seen him for a few days, and we were beginning to hope he'd moved on . . .'

'So we decided we weren't going to talk about Mr High-And-Mighty Konan the Kestrel any more,' Buster bitterly butted in. 'Not to each other, not to anybody. We didn't want to tempt fate, mate. Silly, really.'

'Please don't think too badly of us, Adam,' added Dottie. 'We've been spending our days under . . . *that beast's* shadow, continually wondering if he was poised to swoop. You can't possibly imagine what that's like.'

'Huh! I wouldn't bet on it if I were you,' Adam muttered, and turned his back on the three of them. 'So why don't you just get away from him?' he asked. 'You can fly, can't you? You could escape to anywhere you want.'

'But . . . this is our home, Adam,' said Jen. 'Besides, it doesn't matter where you go,' she added, sadly. 'There's always another Konan.'

'Well, I'm not hanging around to be a meal for *this* particular version,' said Adam. The twisting in his stomach was becoming unbearable. He had to *do* something. 'You lot can stay here if you want. *I'm* leaving.'

He turned round, pushed past his friends, and stomped across the bird-table. They followed, but there was no stopping him. He walked faster and faster, reached the far edge running, raised his wings – and took off.

'Adam, wait!' he heard Jen call out. Adam ignored her.

He raised his tail feathers to give himself more height, enough to clear the circular washing line. Then he quickly dropped to fence level again.

He was just grateful he could see above and in front at the same time.

CHAPTER ELEVEN

A Tough Choice

Adam flew along as quickly as he could, keeping low and trying his best to stay under cover wherever possible. When he had to come out into the open, he scanned the sky above for any menacing black dots.

After a while, he realised he was getting closer to the huge oak tree which stood near his house. He cautiously left the shelter of a bush, zig-zagged swiftly through the air, and finally made it on to a high branch.

Not the topmost one this time, however. Adam thought he would be rather too visible there. He settled instead for a position slightly lower down, close to the trunk, and well concealed by plenty of foliage.

It gave him a pretty good view of the neighbourhood, though. Adam was looking for a certain shimmering, eerie cloud – and there it was, in the distance, behind a row of shops. It definitely wasn't moving, either.

Adam checked the route that would take him to it. There seemed to be enough cover. So to escape

Konan, he just had to fly into the cloud and let it transform him back into a boy. He stepped forward, raised his wings . . .

But then he paused, and dropped them. A familiar set of images had come pushing and shoving into his mind – *Kenny* watching him, *Kenny* chasing him, *Kenny* looming above him at the base of this very tree.

And Kenny would be waiting for him at school on Monday morning.

If he became a human being again that is, Adam thought. He *could* stay as he was and just try to avoid Konan – although that wouldn't be easy, he realised. He would have to be constantly aware, continually on the alert.

But then that was the kind of future he faced with Kenny, wasn't it?

Adam was beginning to understand what characters in movies meant when they said they were stuck between a rock and a hard place. Konan or Kenny? A bird bully, or a human one? It was a tough choice, all right.

Adam's stomach twisted and tightened as he gripped the branch and brooded. Another idea occurred to him. Suppose he used the cloud to become a different bird or animal? He could be anything he wanted!

But that wasn't the answer. What was it Jen had said? *It doesn't matter where you go, there's always another Konan.* Adam knew she was right. There must be dog bullies, cat bullies, mouse bullies, even insect bullies . . .

A nightmare picture flashed into Adam's mind, of

him being pursued by bully, after bully, after bully, even a ridiculous, bulling ant. Suddenly he went hot over over – and that was the moment when everything changed . . .

Adam felt the knot in his stomach pull as tight as it would go, then burst into a blaze of anger. It burned inside him, and soon he felt as if the flames were furiously fanning out and flowing through his whole body.

He was much more angry than he had been with Dottie, Buster and Jen. He was angry with *himself* for being such a wimp. Was he going to spend the rest of his life running away from *anybody* who pushed him around?

It was obviously his weakness, he decided. When he got frightened, his instinct was to take to his heels – or his wings. He hadn't really thought about it before – but now that he did, he could see it didn't solve much.

On the contrary. It had just led him from one bully to another.

It had also meant leaving behind good friends like Craig, and people like his mum and his gran, who both loved him, and great new pals like Dottie, Buster and Jen. Besides, he'd only brought his fear with him.

He knew it was still there, hiding deep within him like some kind of evil parasite, waiting to start tying that knot in his stomach again once his blaze of anger faded. Then suddenly the solution popped into his head.

Maybe he ought to keep his anger burning.

Yes, that was it, he realised, excited to feel the fear shrivel a little. He had to *be* angry, *stay* angry, *use* that anger to stay strong against the bullies. Who did Konan think he *was*, for heaven's sake? How *dare* Konan threaten him!

Adam raised his wings again, then stepped forward and dived off the branch. But instead of making for the small cloud that was shimmering in the distance, he turned – and powered back in the direction he had come.

He had decided it was time to make a stand.

CHAPTER TWELVE
All For One

It took Adam quite a while to find his three friends. They weren't on the bird-table, or the fence where they had played Ins-and-Outies and Sneaky-Beak. He finally decided to try looking in the Ups-and-Downies shed.

He landed on the roof and peeked through one of the holes into the dim, cobwebby interior. He saw Dottie, Buster and Jen immediately. They were huddled together on the handle of an old lawnmower in the corner.

'OK, this is what I think,' Jen was saying. 'We stay inside when it's light, and only go out to look for food at night. That way we *should* be safe.'

'Well, I'm not so sure, Jen,' murmured Dottie, anxiously. 'I'll bet that *that beast* can see perfectly in the dark. I wouldn't put anything past him.'

'Neither would I,' muttered Buster, gloomily. 'Besides, it won't be much of a life, will it? Stuck in here terrified all day, no real flying, no games . . .'

'But there's nothing else we can *do*,' said Jen,

desperately. 'Is there?'

'I've got a suggestion,' said Adam, suddenly flying down from the roof and perching beside them.

Buster and Jen turned in surprise, and Dottie leapt off the handle into the air in a frantic flurry of feathers and squawks.

'Adam!' said Jen, obviously delighted. 'You came back!'

'Yes, and that's twice you've nearly given me heart failure,' said Dottie crossly, landing again. 'Must you *always* make such a dramatic entrance?'

'Oh, be quiet, Dottie,' said Buster. 'You're a sight for sore eyes, mate, and no mistake,' he said to Adam. 'What's this suggestion of yours, then?'

'It's very simple,' said Adam, quietly. He was still filled with plenty of that hot, burning anger. 'I suggest . . . *I* stand up to Konan instead.'

Three beaks fell open in unison, and there was a stunned silence.

'Er . . . no offence, mate,' said Buster at last, 'but are you feeling all right?'

'Poor bird!' said Dottie, tragically, *'That beast* has driven him mad!'

'Come on, Adam,' said Jen, softly. 'You can't be serious – can you?'

'But I am,' said Adam, fiercely, looking at each of his friends in turn. 'I swear to you, I've never been more serious about anything in my life.'

Adam had done a lot of thinking during his flight from the oak tree. He was *determined* to take on Konan, and stop him making his friends' lives a total misery – if he could. Adam had realised it was a tall order, though.

Konan was powerful and strong, and seemed utterly invincible to the small birds he lorded it over. But then Adam began to wonder if maybe he wasn't so great after all. If maybe there was a tiny chink in is armour.

If maybe he was like Adam – and had a weakness.

The more he had thought about it, the more Adam believed he might have hit on something. It didn't even have to be a major weakness, just a

flaw of some kind that he could exploit to their advantage.

'So let me get this absolutely straight,' said Jen eventually, glancing uneasily at Dottie and Buster. 'You're going to *spy* on Konan. And you think that will help you to work out a plan to stop him bullying us.'

'I can't really give you any guarantees,' Adam replied. 'But yes, that's it, more or less. Now I just need you to tell me where I can find him.'

'I see,' said Jen, thoughtfully. 'Would you excuse us for a moment?'

'Er . . . no problem,' said Adam, puzzled.

Jen turned to Dottie and Buster and pulled them into a huddle. Adam could hear heated whispering, but not what the three of them were actually saying, although both Dottie and Buster seemed rather unhappy.

Eventually the huddle broke up, and Jen turned to face Adam again.

'We've decided we simply can't allow you to do this by yourself,' she announced, firmly. Both Dottie and Buster opened their beaks to speak, but Jen quelled them with a stern look. 'So – you can count *us* in too.'

'I . . . I don't know what to say,' murmured Adam, his eyes prickling.

'I do,' said Buster. 'And I'd better say it before Dottie and I change our minds. Wingsies! he said, suddenly putting a wing forward. 'One for all . . .'

Jen and Dottie each put a wing forward as well, and three tips touched. Adam added his wing tip to theirs – then four small birds spoke in unison.

'. . . *And all for one!*'

CHAPTER THIRTEEN
Now or Never

They left the shed, and Adam's friends led him in a new direction. After a few moments they entered a dark, dark wood, and kept going until they reached its far edge. Beyond the trees was a patch of open waste ground.

Dottie, Buster and Jen settled on a branch which afforded plenty of cover, and Adam joined them. His friends nodded, then turned to peer through the leaves. Adam did the same – and drew in his breath sharply.

Slap bang in the middle of the waste ground was an old, thick post. Perched arrogantly on top of it, preening his chest feathers with that cruel, vicious beak – was Mr High-and-Mighty Konan the Kestrel himself!

'Ssssh!' the others hissed crossly at Adam together. 'He'll hear you!

'Sorry! Adam whispered back, and settled down to watch his enemy. Seeing him made it easy for Adam to keep his anger burning brightly . . .

It seemed that this was where Koran invariably returned between his hunting patrols over the neighbourhood. It was a perfect place to observe him, and Adam was able to watch Konan take off and land repeatedly.

Nevertheless, Adam insisted on changing position – twice. It was worth it as well, despite Buster's grumbles and Dottie's moans. It gave Adam the opportunity to watch Konan flying through different kinds of airspace.

And gradually, Adam acquired a picture of the kestrel's abilities.

Konan was certainly very strong, and fast once he actually got going. He also had a particularly nasty party trick that seemed to give him a great deal of pleasure. He *loved* swooping from height on unsuspecting prey.

The four friends didn't enjoy watching him do it, though.

But Adam soon realised Konan *did* have a weakness, if only a slight one. Because of his large wingspan,

Konan wasn't so good at low-level pursuit of somebody mobile, especially where there were lots of obstacles.

Suddenly Adam found himself thinking of Road Running and Wile E. Coyote, the cartoon characters he'd seen on TV at his gran's place earlier that day.

Wile E. Coyote pursued Road Runner and usually ended up falling over a cliff or crashing into some obstacle, didn't he? And that was because he always lost his temper and stopped concentrating on what he was doing.

Adam focused on Konan once more, and thought hard. A plan started to form in his mind. A low-level chase . . . plenty of taunting and teasing . . . Konan being made to lose *his* temper . . . and ending up in a deadly trap.

Adam knew just the one, too.

He also knew it was a case of now or never. If he sat there working out the details and trying to persuade himself he could succeed, the fear would probably return, and he'd be finished. And that simply wasn't an option.

So he pushed straight through the leaves – and took off. He flew a little way into the open space between the wood and Konan on his post, then hovered, beating his wings noisily. Konan didn't appear to notice.

'Adam!' hissed Jen, desperately. 'What are you *doing?*'

'Hey, Konan, you big, ugly lump!' Adam yelled, ignoring her.

'Oh, terrific!' Adam heard Buster muttering. 'Some plan *this* is turning out to be. He shouts, Konan eats us, all our worries are over, right?'

'Konan!' yelled Adam, more loudly. 'Has anyone ever told you how stupid you look sitting there like that? Or how badly your breath smells?'

'It hasn't been such a bad life really,' Adam heard Dottie whimpering. 'So I mustn't complain. Is he coming yet? I c-c-can't bear to look . . .'

'*KONAN!*' yelled Adam, more loudly still. 'You'd better be listening to me, you dozy fat twit, because I've got something important to say.'

A deep silence fell over the waste ground. Konan slowly turned his great head until those scary, black eyes were fixed firmly on Adam. But this time Adam managed to keep himself under complete control.

'Well, well,' said Konan, coldly. 'If it isn't little blue snack. You're a tad early . . . and what could *you* possibly have to say that's important?'

'Just this, dimbo . . .' Adam replied. *'BET YOU CAN'T CATCH ME!'*

Then he turned – and flew off like a bat out of hell.

CHAPTER FOURTEEN
A Close Shave

For the second time that day, Adam was grateful he had all-round vision. He flew quickly along the edge of the wood, searching for a gap he could dive into. But he made certain he knew what was happening behind him.

Konan had immediately risen from his post, and was steadily gaining height as he pursued him. The kestrel was waiting for the best moment to swoop, thought Adam. So the sooner he got under cover, the better.

Adam saw a gap and swung into it. He flew through the trees, dodging trunks and branches lit by sunbeams slanting through the green canopy. He could see the figure of Konan flickering above it, keeping pace with him.

Adam emerged from the wood and made for the gardens. He was in full sunlight now, and the contrast dazzled him momentarily, making him lose sight of the kestrel. Oh no, he thought, instantly feeling very vulnerable . . .

Suddenly Konan swooped, his dark, evil shape dropping swiftly from the sky, those razor-sharp talons glint-

ing. Adam thought he was dead meat . . . but then three small figures seemed to appear from nowhere.

Dottie, Buster and Jen swept between Adam and Konan, startling the kestrel and making him miss his target, although it was a close shave. Konan reared back in mid-air, beating his wings furiously, and HISSED.

'Don't stop, Adam!' shouted Jen. 'We'll be all right!'

Adam didn't need to be told twice. He dodged into

the nearest garden, and his enemy was soon pursuing him again. But Adam felt safer weaving between greenhouses and bushes, knowing Konan was at a disadvantage.

'Hurry up, slowcoach!' Adam called out. He could see Konan was getting more and more angry. 'You'll *never* catch me at this rate!'

'Why, I'll rip you to shreds . . .' Konan spluttered.

Adam took no notice. He concentrated on the gardens they were flying through, because now he was coming to the tricky part. He had spotted what he was aiming at – three gardens ahead, two gardens ahead, one . . .

And here it was, the circular washing line, still crowded with clothes thank goodness, thought Adam. He slowed down enough to let Konan get a little closer.

That big, cruel beak snapped viciously at his tail feathers . . .

Then Adam flew on at top speed, infuriating his pursuer. Adam dived towards the washing, folded his wings in, tucked his own beak into his chest . . . and *WHIZZED* clean through, exactly as he had done before.

He heard a loud . . . *CRASH!* behind him, then shot out the other side. He made a perfect landing on the bird-table, and turned to look at the washing line. It jerked and twitched and jumped as if it had suddenly come alive.

Or as if something alive had seen it too late . . . and got stuck inside.

Adam took off, and cautiously flew over it. He landed next to a peg on the outermost ring, and peered down. And there below him, trapped in the sleeves and straps and folds of the wet clothes, was a furious Konan.

'Just you wait til I get out of here,' he hissed as he struggled and thrashed and strained. 'You'll be sorry you were ever hatched, you . . .'

'And what makes you think you're *going* to get out?' asked Adam.

Konan went still as he absorbed the full impact of Adam's words. At that moment, Dottie, Buster and Jen arrived. They settled on the washing line next to Adam, and stared open-beaked at their imprisoned tormentor.

'Are you OK, Adam?' said Jen at last.

'Yes, I am,' Adam replied.' Although I'm pretty sure I *wouldn't* be if it hadn't been for you three. Thanks for diving in like that and helping me.'

'No problem, mate,' said Buster, proudly. 'That's what friends are for.'

'Psst, Adam,' whispered Dottie, nervously, 'What about . . . *him*?'

She nodded meaningfully in the kestrel's direction. The four small birds peered down. A large, black, rather worried-looking eye peered back at them from inside a tangled blouse.

Adam knew what Dottie meant. What should they do with Konan now the kestrel was at their mercy? It was a question Adam hadn't considered until then. But suddenly, as his anger faded, he saw *everything* clearly.

'Right, Konan,' he said, calmly. 'Listen to me carefully. Here's the deal . . .'

CHAPTER FIFTEEN
Moving On

It was very simple. Adam told Konan they could leave him trapped in the washing, or Adam could arrange to have him set free – on one condition. The kestrel would have to agree to quit the neighbourhood – for ever.

'Why, that's *ridiculous*,' spat Konan, and started struggling again. But he only succeeded in making his bonds tighter, and Adam could see he was weakening, too. 'You can't dictate terms to *me*, he splattered. I am Konan the Kestrel . . .'

'Suit yourself,' said Adam. 'But don't be surprised if we tell everybody else you've been terrorising where they might find you. I'd expect quite a few *peckish* visitors if I were you. Come on,' he said to his friends.

'Wait a minute!' the kestrel squeaked, desperately. Adam paused, and looked down at him. 'Er . . . perhaps I *have* been rather hasty,' said Konan, contritely. 'I'll do whatever you want. *JUST GET ME OUT OF HERE!*'

'OK, Konan,' Adam replied happily. 'I'm glad you're being sensible . . .'

A few moments later, Adam and his friends landed on the roof of the Ups-and-Downies shed once more. Dottie, Buster and Jen couldn't praise Adam enough, and he stood there feeling very, very good about himself.

But he did feel sad as well. Adam had realised he would have to become human to arrange for Konan to be set free. How else could he phone the RSPCA and tell them a kestrel was trapped in a washing line?

They were bound to release Konan, but Adam reckoned the kestrel would stick to their deal. He'd almost certainly be reluctant to remain in a neighbourhood where a mere budgie could call on *human* assistance.

There was something else, too. It *had* all been a terrific adventure, and of course he would miss Dottie, Buster and Jen. But Adam had also realised now he *wanted* to return to his old life. It was time to go home.

'Listen, Adam,' said Jen eventually. 'What you did today was *fantastic*, but you mustn't put yourself in any more danger. We know you were only trying to fool Konan with that stuff about getting him out of there . . .'

'Actually, I wasn't,' said Adam, 'I *can* do it – although it's impossible to explain,' Jen opened her beak to speak, but Adam wouldn't let her. 'It's some-

thing I have to do alone, I'm afraid. And then I'll be, er . . . moving on.'

'Oh, what a shame! said Dottie. 'We could have had such fun!'

'Yeah, sorry you've got to go, mate! said Buster, 'It's been great!'

'We will see you again, though,' Jen asked, quietly. 'Won't we?'

'Er . . . I should think so,' Adam replied. Not that they would be able to recognise him, he thought sadly as he raised his wings. 'Anyway, take care of your-selves,' he said, silently wishing them long, safe lives. 'Bye!'

'Bye, Adam!' they chirped in unison. 'You take care too!' added Jen.

Adam watched his three friends grow smaller and smaller as he gained height. After a while he lost sight of them, and concentrated on heading for the oak tree, where he landed to search for a certain shimmering cloud.

It hadn't moved from where he's seen it earlier, and soon he was flying into it, his mind filled with images of how he looked normally. The bizarre sensations were exactly the same, although they came in reverse order . . .

At last the transformation seemed to have finished. Adam hardly dared look at himself, but when he did, he breathed a sigh of relief. He checked himself over from head to toes, and everything was just as it should be.

Adam looked around, and realised he was in the narrow alley behind the sweet-shop he visited with Craig. Adam walked to the end of it, and turned into the street beyond. The shimmering cloud had completely disappeared.

He had already decided he was going to keep the whole thing a secret. He hadn't been himself even before he'd been transformed into a budgie, and he didn't want everybody he knew to think he'd finally cracked up.

Because he hadn't. He was strong – strong enough to defeat a bully who was much scarier than Kenny could ever be. Besides, thought Adam, when it had come to it, Kenny hadn't seemed a particularly *confident* bully . . .

Suddenly, as he turned the corner into his street, Adam realised dealing with Kenny on Monday would be a doddle. He was looking forward to it.

He also realised he was absolutely famished, and broke into a run.

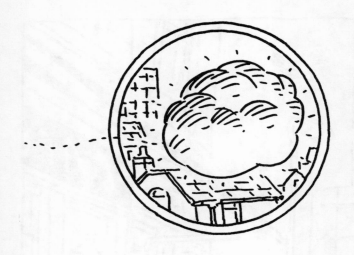

A small cloud of gas drifts high above an oak tree . . .
And a boy settles down happily to eat his tea.
Where the cloud will drift next is a mystery. Perhaps it will
waft its way into the secret heart of a dark wood.
Perhaps it will shimmer eerily through a supermarket . . .
Whatever the truth, one thing is certain. Any
child who meets it is in for an amazing experience,
as one particular boy discovered. And next
time it might be you tumbling into the weird, wild
and wonderful world of . . . **Swoppers!**